T0132239

Quest for a Family Pet

Written by
Sonya Correll Cook

Illustrated by
Devora Transou
and Karen Watkins

Character Development
by Tyler D. Cook

AuthorHouse™
1663 Liberty Drive
Bloomington, IN 47403
www.authorhouse.com
Phone: 833-262-8899

Because of the dynamic nature of the Internet, any web addresses or links contained in this book may have changed
since publication and may no longer be valid. The views expressed in this work are solely those of the author and do
not necessarily reflect the views of the publisher, and the publisher hereby disclaims any responsibility for them.

Any people depicted in stock imagery provided by Getty Images are models,
and such images are being used for illustrative purposes only.
Certain stock imagery © Getty Images.

This book is printed on acid-free paper.

ISBN: 978-1-4343-5043-5 (sc)
ISBN: 978-1-4817-2070-0 (e)

Library of Congress Control Number: 2008900712

Print information available on the last page.

Published by AuthorHouse 10/11/2022

authorHOUSE®

Dear Parents:

Mothers and fathers everywhere would love the perfect scenario for their children including a mother, father, siblings, pets, a wonderful home, and maybe even a white picket fence. But the truth is that a family is simply individuals coming together to create a oneness in love.

As my children and I grow day by day, through pains and victories, we have discovered that we are different from most families and yet similar to many. And although each member of our family is different, we accept, and learn from one another just the same. With the blessing of my children, I decided to share my family with you.

My vision and motivation is simply this …..

No matter what the makeup of your family is or how it came to be….Family is still simply…… life, love and lessons.

I am thrilled to welcome you to, "The Adventures of Nique, Nick, and Nelle." Through this collection of short stories, I hope that, together, your family will learn valuable lessons about diversity, acceptance, responsibility, togetherness and more. As you join this adventure, think about what makes your family unique and what you learn together. You can even write your own family journal. We all have family adventures!

Our adventure begins as Nique, Nick and Nelle try to convince me that they are ready for their first pet! Get ready….get set…lets go!

Joyfully,

Sonya C. Cook
Author
"Lessons learned through laughter are not easily forgotten".

My name is Dominique Coker. Everyone calls me Nique (pronounced NEEK). I am ten years old and the coolest, most good looking, and modest big brother around! My mom says that I'm a clown, but no circus is good enough for me. I just think she's jealous because I am the best practical joker in town! My younger brother, Nick, is 8 and I have a 7 year old sister, Nelle. My parents are divorced and we live with my mom. My mom is a firm believer of saying what you mean and meaning what you say. She can be so funny and pretty cool too…at times.

We don't have any pets, well, not any 'real' pets anyway. Mom says that she doesn't need another mouth to feed and another body to clean up after. Last summer, we felt sure that we could handle all of the responsibilities that came along with a puppy. We begged mom for a puppy. Oh man how we begged! We thought she was about to cave in. Especially when we all gave mom the puppy dog eyes as we danced around and sang "Pleeeeeze!" But we didn't stop there. We gave mom a list of responsibilities and who would carry out each one. When she didn't cave in, we became desperate. Mom left us no choice but to send in our Secret Weapon--Nelle.

Whenever we want something that we knew mom wouldn't go for, we first lay the ground work, then send Nelle in for the kill. She's the cute, spoiled, baby girl, and she can talk mom into things we never thought would fly.

Nelle climbed up on mom's lap, gave her a big hug, put her face close to mom's lips so she could kiss Nelle's juicy right cheek, and sweetly asked mom again. Mom didn't say yes, but she didn't say no. And in our book, that's success! We settled for "I'll think about it." Then we quickly retreated back to our bedroom to plot our next move. We kept our rooms clean, didn't argue with each other, and made sure that we didn't get on her nerves. We even volunteered for extra chores. Now you know we had to want a dog pretty bad to do that!

ust when we were about to bust from holding in our curiosity, mom proudly announced
at the time has come. We all showered her with kisses and hugs. Then Nick, the dramatic
ne, cleared his throat. Mom, Nelle, and I looked at each other and plopped down on the
ouch.

ick stood directly in front of mom and placed his hand on her shoulder. As humbly as he
ould, he began 'the speech'. "Mom, mom, mom, I know I speak for all of us when I say
at you are the best mom on earth. We know how much you sacrifice to supply all of our
eeds and some of our wants. Mom, we truly appreciate everything you've done for us.
e know that it's not easy being a single mom with three children these days. We realize
at you give us things that we don't even need and definitely don't deserve." I quickly
eared my throat before he blew it. He gave me the eye and brought his speech to a close.
We love you mom, and just couldn't let this moment slip away without letting you know
ow much we love and appreciate you". That was our cue. Nelle and I quickly jumped up
nd joined Nick and mom in a group hug.

Mom pretended to wipe tears from her eyes as she opened the door to the garage. As soon as we thought she couldn't hear us, we gave each other a high five and began our victory dance. Mission Accomplished...or was it?

When mom opened the door, Nick and Nelle jumped down on the floor so that they could greet the newest member of our family. I fell over the end of the couch straining to hear the pitter-patter of little feet on the kitchen floor. I knew instantly that something was wrong when all I heard was the clicking of mom's church shoes.

Mom proudly strolled into the living room with one hand behind her back. Being the brains of this outfit, I think I popped a blood vessel trying to figure out what kind of puppy could she hold behind her back with one hand. A smile crept across mom's face. Not just any smile, but a 'don't-even-think-for-one-minute-you-can-outsmart-me smile'. At that point, I knew something stunk, and it definitely wasn't a puppy!

Mom began the second part of her performance. "Kids, you know that I love you more than anything on this earth. And nothing warms my heart more than to shower my babies with gifts. You guys have really been good these past couple of weeks. You know my job is stressful this time of year. But you have been very considerate and understanding…" Mom continued her speech but I didn't hear any of it. I was still trying to figure out what she had behind her back. The Oscar for "Best Performance to a Captive Audience" goes to…..

Suddenly, mom clapped her hands. We heard a bark! But where was it coming from? We jumped up and looked around for our long awaited new best friend! Then we heard a whimper and two more barks! Nelle squealed, "Mommy, where is it?" Mom giggled and said that she didn't hear anything. We pounced on her like chicken gravy on white rice and tickled her until she surrendered.

She's so pretty when she laughs. Her smile is as bright as the sun on a fresh spring morning, and her cheeks bunch up like Nelle's. And you can't help but notice how her eyes sparkle when she's happy.

As we followed her into the kitchen, she explained that the puppy already knew tricks. But he was a little shy. She told us to be patient and give the puppy time to get used to us. Then mom opened the pantry door. There it sat, wagging its tail. It was the cutest Chow puppy I had ever seen. It was white as snow, with floppy ears, and eyes black as coal. I couldn't believe it. After all of the pleading, acts of kindness, and extra chores, mom finally rewarded us with a puppy!

Wait a minute! There's that smell again. And it wasn't the scent of a new puppy! Nick noticed that the puppy made stiff movements. Nelle squealed when she touched it. I looked at mom sitting at the kitchen table. She winked and began to laugh. She didn't just giggle, she laughed so hard that she had to run to the bathroom to keep from wetting her pants! I picked up the dog and shook my head. It was some kind of stuffed mechanical dog. While Nick and Nelle were trying to break down the bathroom door, I sat in the kitchen floor and began to laugh. She got us. Boy, she got us good!

Actually, the dog is pretty cool. We named him Snowball. When we questioned mom about buying us a mechanical dog, she just played dumb and said that we didn't tell her we wanted a "REAL" puppy. Then she kissed us on the forehead and began to make dinner.

My mom is pretty strict about meal time. She says that a family that eats together works together, plays together, and prays together, stays together. So she makes sure that we eat at least one meal a day together. We all pitch in with setting the table, preparing drinks, and helping mom take the food to the table. Mom's a pretty good cook. Whenever Nick and I are at the table, there are seldom leftovers.

During dinner, mom explained that she didn't mean to disappoint us. She just knew how bad we wanted a puppy, so she bought a pet that would suit the needs of our family. We are a very active family. I play football, Nick plays basketball, and Nelle is into gymnastics and cheerleading. Mom works fulltime and sings in two church choirs. So we are not home enough to give a real pet all the love and care it deserves. When she explained it to us, we admitted she made the right choice. Snowball is the perfect pet for us.

Mom, Nelle, Nick, and I played with Snowball for hours after dinner. Snowball ca
perform several tricks. He can raise his paw to shake your hand, sit up, beg, snore
and chew on his bone! That's more than a lot of real dogs can do.

You know, I'm not mad at my mom for playing that trick on us. We asked for a pupp
and she gave us a puppy. After all, we knew deep down inside that we weren't read
for a real pet. She just didn't have to play us like that!

Reading Guide for Quest for a Family Pet

Children need as much practice as possible to help them excel with reading comprehension. Reading comprehension is not a skill which develops overnight. In order to master this skill, it takes constant practice and determination from both children and parents. Use this reading guide to help facilitate reading comprehension practice for your child. Refer to the page numbers to help your child reference the text to find and locate answers.

Vocabulary

Prior to reading the story with your child, review the following vocabulary words to help them better understand the story.

quest: (cover) a hunt or search for something
desperate (page 3): to have a strong need or want
curiosity (page 5): a form of the word **curious**; to be interested in knowing
surrendered (page 9): a form of the word **surrender**; to give up or let go
pleading (page 10): a form of the word **plead**; to beg or insist
mechanical (page 10): an non living object made from metal parts

Reading Comprehension Questions

Use the following questions to help your child comprehend the story. These questions can be answered as the story is read, or afterwards as review.

1. On page 3, what do you think the speaker meant by saying they became desperate?

2. Why did the Nique call Nelle their 'Secret Weapon'? (page 3)

3. What is a secret weapon? (page 3)

4. On page 4, why do you think the kids are willing to settle for "I'll think about it" from their mom?

5. According to page 6, why do you think the kids thought their mission was accomplished?

6. On page 9, how does the speaker describe how the children pounce on their mother?

7. What does the speaker use to compare his mother's smile? (page 9)

8. How does the speaker describe the puppy? (page 10)

9. What clues tell you the family was not ready for a puppy?

10. How do the children feel at the end of the story?

11. How would you feel if this happened to you?

This book is dedicated to my children,
Tyler DomiNIQUE, Ryan NICKolas, and Chelsea DaNiELLE

Thanks for the laughter, the lessons, and the love.

Love always,

Mom

Printed in the United States
by Baker & Taylor Publisher Services